Celebrity Crushes

Poetic Woman

CELEBRITY CRUSHES

This book is written to provide information and motivation to readers. Its purpose is not to render any type of psychological, legal, or professional advice of any kind. The content is the sole opinion and expression of the author, and not necessarily that of the publisher.

Credits

Photo of Charlie Wilson, by Cees van der Pol

Printed in the United States of America.

ISBN   978-1-64552-079-5   (Paperback)
ISBN   978-1-64552-080-1   (Digital)

Lettra Press books may be ordered through booksellers or by contacting:

Lettra Press LLC
18229 E 52nd Ave.
Denver City, CO 80249
1 303 586 1431 | info@lettrapress.com
www.lettrapress.com

Preface

Throughout my journey as a writer, I would like to thank my fellow friends. I would like to thank my junior high writing teacher Mrs. Joseph for giving me that extra push to keep practicing my writing. My high school drama teacher Mr. Cuhran for inspiring me to write about all things drama-filled. Then you have my friend Carla T that I consider as my sister-in-law. She inspired me to want to write stage plays. Finally, you have my friend Authoress Terry Lyle one of my biggest fans that believes in my success.

Table of Contents

Dedication page

I dedicate this book to my fellow writers. Authoress Terry Lyle, Author Jewelze & Denisha Burgess.

Chapter 1

As an iconic R&B soulful singer, Charlie Wilson lives up to his name "cool uncle." A man that no man could ever measure up to. Someone that reflects on his weakness and makes them stronger. An artist that's been in the music industry for over four decades. An artist that has many number one singles and also should have been nominated for other awards.

Furthermore, though diagnosed with prostate cancer years ago he stood strong and beat it. He took immediate action and went to the doctor right away. And right now to this day he still has his wife by side every step of the way. Unlike most other women they would've taken the sickness as a sign. A warning to be prepared to collect the insurance money and bounce.

Even up to this point, every Charlie Wilson fan enjoys going to see him perform live in concert. Wishing that he would walk up to them and sing to them. Make them weal to the knees. Fantasizing about what they would say if they got the chance to shake his hand. Dreaming about collaborating with him on a music track. Or even what it would be like to own a sweat towel of his.

Personally of all of Charlie Wilson's accomplishments, I'm surprised that he hasn't starred in any movies. Besides having a day named after him, he personally need his own apparel line. Just imagine if Charlie Wilson had his own apparel line how it would be a hit like his music, hats and t-shirts. You would see every Charlie Wilson fan arguing over whom going to buy the last pair of Charlie Wilson shoes.

With being a songwriter and producer being his talent I dis-respect those that dis-respect the art of music. Which in tail is why I barely even talk to some of my co-workers that like to use the term "old-heads." I had to set them straight and tell them that I love old school music and who cares if you have a problem with that. Which in terms is why you can't keep a man to begin with? Maybe listening to Charlie Wilson music could teach you a thing or two about relationships alone.

Chapter 2

Test your music knowledge and you'll know whether or not you have C.W.S.

1). What is Charlie Wilson's zodiac sign?

a). Aquarius

b). pieces

c). Libra

d). none of the above

2). How many cd's has T-swang released to this day?

a). 3

b). 5

c). 6

3). How many books has Authoress
    Terry Lyle had published so far?

a). 4

b). 7

c). 8

4). Would you as a fan be willing
    to go to jail for trespassing on a
    celebrity's property?

a). yes I have the bail money

b). no I can't afford a lawyer

c). no it 's not that serious

5). What was Whitney Houston's
    favorite color?

a). yellow

b). lavender

c). blue

6). Is it okay to name your child after
a famous person?

a). yes you like there name

b). no you have some other unique
name in mind

c). you'll just name them after a car
you like instead

7). Is it okay to get a celebrity's name
tattooed on you if you're not related
to them?

a). no that 's obsession

b). yes you don't care what anyone
thinks

c). no your next mate won't like it

8). Who does Jahiem dedicate his
    "Florida" song on his latest album?

a). Trayvon Martin

b). one of his friends

c). one of his family members

9). What's the name of Authoress Terry
    Lyle's new show?

a). authoress corner

b). you don't know

c). blogstalk radio

10). Would you be willing to pay $100k
     to have any celebrity host a live
     concert?

a). yes you'll raise the money

b). no you have bills to pay

c). no you just put the last $3 in the
   gas tank

. Answers are on the next page

Answers

1). a

2). B

3). C

4). C

5). B

6). B

7). A

8). A

9). C

10). A

Chapter 3

From entertainers to show-stoppers celebrities are well known artists from all walks of the earth. Entertaining millions of fans and inspiring some to follow in their footsteps. Receiving instagram messages like, "could you hook me up on your label?"

Knowing the right people in the music industry is sometimes just mythical. Having skills, a degree and the knowledge to move forward might get you one foot in the door. Rejection is just part of the process. But, you just have to take rejection and turn it into something positive.

Listening to oh! You'll never amount to anything will stir you in the wrong direction. Trust and believe most entertainers are afraid to love. They don't know if a person is there to love them for them. Or to just see what they can get out of them.

All of the money in the world wouldn't matter if I was a celebrity. Having my one true love is all that friend no matter the situation. But two of my writing mentors believe that I can become a well-known writer. Thanks Mrs. Joseph and Authoress Terry Lyle for believing in me.

So, without further a due I'm going to introduce some show-stoppers.

Bad entertainment dance team which consists of 35 members. Their coach and choreographer is someone known as "DJ Bad." And his wife is Mrs. Bad. Both of which are my oldest son grandparents. Then you have the members of Boyz II Men. Finally you have T-Swang who can dance and sing and whose music is club-banging.

.BAD ENTERTAINMENT DANCE TEAM

performing at the mall

. Boyz II Men members & the owners of Bad entertainment (Mr. & Mrs. Bad Entertainment).

.T-Swang getting ready for a performance show

Chapter 4

17

CELEBRITY CRUSH 101

LADY G's Celebrity Crush

My celebrity crush is too good to be true. I go by the method of a writer doesn't reveal her own celebrity crush. Just know what if you put two and two together you might figure it out. On that note, I leave you with these words "for the love of R&B music, what will it make a woman do?"

AUTHORESS TERRY LYLE'S CELEBRITY CRUSH

"My crush is on Marvin Sapp, mainly because he's a Godly man, very nice and down to earth and that brother can sing makes me weak in the knees."

JAZZY J'S CELEBRITY CRUSH

"My crush is on Yo Gotti cause he fine as ever!! And he a hard rapper.

AUTHOR JEWELZE'S CELEBRITY CRUSH

"My crush is on T.G.T. cause they are triple the threat when it comes to sexiness in the music game. Idris Elba well he's just damn sexy.

DIRTY DIVA'S CELEBRITY CRUSH

"My crush is on Idris Elba mainly cause I love everything about him."

POETRY SECTION

Celebrity Crush

I have a celebrity crush and I'm

Really over the edge.

I got strangely caught up because I have lost my head.

Looking a the glitz's and wanting to be a part of it.

So I'm stalking on you secretly because I think we would fit.

But I'm sick in my mind because I took it too far.

I showed up at your house now locked behind bars.

Now my silly ass thought we had a future.

After threatening you and being abusive.

It's okay to admire your dream.

But keep it in perspective if you know what I mean.

A celebrity crush can go too far.

Especially if you foolishly disregard the law.

Written by Authoress Terry Lyle

As I Lay

As I lay asleep and dream.

Dream of how some celebrities eat their ice-cream.

Dream of how celebrities live their life day by day.

Sometimes taking a look at mines wishing it was that way.

How some celebrities don't always get the credit that they deserve?

When it terms some women try to put their bid in to reserve.

How they have a reputation to uphold?

But when they play their cards right good things always unfold.

How the good ones appreciate their fan-base?

But trust and believe I'll never lose that race.

Groupies know your place
    Groupies know your place
so your fate is not waste.
    Always doing things you
should not do in haste.
    Now I see you starting to
become a big problem.
    So I would think by now
you shouldn't even bother.
    So groupies know your
place . . .

    Written by Authoress Terry
Lyle

8 don't of a celebrity fan

1). Don't harass them with fan-mail

2). Don't ask them to marry you

3). don't tell them you love them

4). don't instagram one of their band members

5). don't exchange phone numbers with one of their band members

6). don't show up at their door step unannounced

7). don't offer to cook dinner for them

8). don't ask them to be your baby daddy

. Follow these 8 rules and you'll be saving yourself bail money and a restraint order.

Trespass

Trespass on my property once I'll give you a pass.

You try me twice you might find a brick thrown thru your glass.

Go for strike three I'll x you out.

Bring a friend and you'll both meet my little taser for sure no doubt.

Make a will out with your man.

Rest assure I'll knock you out with a frying pan.

Trespass and talk about my past.

I thought for sure our friendship would always last.

Break my heart and tear me down.

Rest assure don't forget you're in my town.

Making my kind of money might drive you wild.

I'll have you dreaming so hard you'll see your inner child.

Treat me with respect and I'll do the same.

Dis-respect me if you want like it 's a game.

Trust in the end you'll be the only one to blame.

Chocolate milk drops

Chocolate milk drops.

Lips taste as good as strawberry lollipops.

A voice which makes me weak to the knees.

With a banging body to match got me biting the pillow and screaming please.

Triple the action. Three times the threat.

The harder you make love the harder you'll sweat.

Pieces of rose petals led to the shower.

As I reach the highest point of ecstasy you know you control the power.

The strength to make love.

Chest as supple as a turtle dove.

Wrap me in your arms and never let go.

Tell me I'm your only woman and how much you love me so.

Massage my body from head to toe.

Put hickies all over my body and never tell anyone you did so.

Put hickies all over my body and never tell anyone you did so.

Chocolate milk drops.

Make love to me until the music stops.

About the author

Victoria Kirby is an inspiring screenwriter who longs for the day to meet her favorite R&B celebrity. She's someone who takes her inspirations and turns them into stories. A woman who stands by her companion side no matter what. Who like no other defends the people that she has respect for? Whether it's her children or another family member. Or even if it's a close friend that she's known for a long time. Her motivation to finish her stories makes the challenge all worthwhile in the end.